For Steven, Casey, and Rachel, who loved to count sleeps. —M.B.P.

For Daniel, Annie, and Neil; thank you for all of your support, patience, and those lovely cups of tea! —S.B.

STERLING CHILDREN'S BOOKS
New York

An Imprint of Sterling Publishing Co., Inc.
1166 Avenue of the Americas
New York, NY 10036

Text © 2017 by Marjorie Blain Parker
Illustrations © 2017 by Sophie Burrows

ISBN 978-1-4549-2060-1

Distributed in Canada by Sterling Publishing Co., Inc.
C/o Canadian Manda Group, 664 Annette Street
Toronto, Ontario, Canada M6S 2C8
Distributed in the United Kingdom by GMC Distribution Services
Castle Place, 166 High Street, Lewes, East Sussex, England BN7 1XU
Distributed in Australia by NewSouth Books
45 Beach Street, Coogee, NSW 2034, Australia

For information about custom editions, special sales, and premium and corporate purchases, please contact Sterling
Special Sales at 800-805-5489 or specialsales@sterlingpublishing.com.

Manufactured in China

Lot #:
2 4 6 8 10 9 7 5 3 1
05/17

www.sterlingpublishing.com

Designed by Heather Kelly
The artwork for this book was created with watercolor and colored pencil.

Kindergarten Countdown!

10 MORE SLEEPS UNTIL SCHOOL STARTS!

by MARJORIE BLAIN PARKER
illustrated by SOPHIE BURROWS

STERLING CHILDREN'S BOOKS

New York

10 more sleeps!

Only **10** more sleeps!

I'll wear new clothes
from my head to my toes.
Kindergarten starts in 10 more sleeps.

9 more sleeps!

Only **9** more sleeps!

I'll fill my pack
with Buddy and a snack.
Kindergarten starts in 9 more sleeps.

8 more sleeps!

Only 8 more sleeps!
I'll ride the bus,
wave goodbye without a fuss.
Kindergarten starts in 8 more sleeps.

7 more sleeps!

(That's the same as a week.)

I'll find the door,
join a circle on the floor.
Kindergarten starts in **7** more sleeps.

Only **6** more sleeps!
I'll make a tag,
say a pledge to the flag.
Kindergarten starts in **6** more sleeps.

5 more sleeps!

Only 5 more sleeps!
I'll paint and glue,
draw a picture or two.
Kindergarten starts in 5 more sleeps.

4 more sleeps!

Only **4** more sleeps!
I'll read a book.
(Well—I'll listen and look.)
Kindergarten starts in **4** more sleeps.

3 more sleeps!

Only **3** more sleeps!

I'll swing and slide
when recess is outside.
Kindergarten starts in **3** more sleeps.

2 more sleeps!

Only 2 more sleeps!
I'll eat my lunch—
cheese to nibble, grapes to munch.
Kindergarten starts in 2 more sleeps.

1 more sleep!

I'm too *excited* to sleep!
I'll make a friend,
who likes to play pretend.
Kindergarten starts in **1** more sleep.

0 more sleeps!

Finally—0 more sleeps!

I wore new clothes!

I filled my pack!

I rode the bus—
it was yellow and black!

SCHOOL BUS

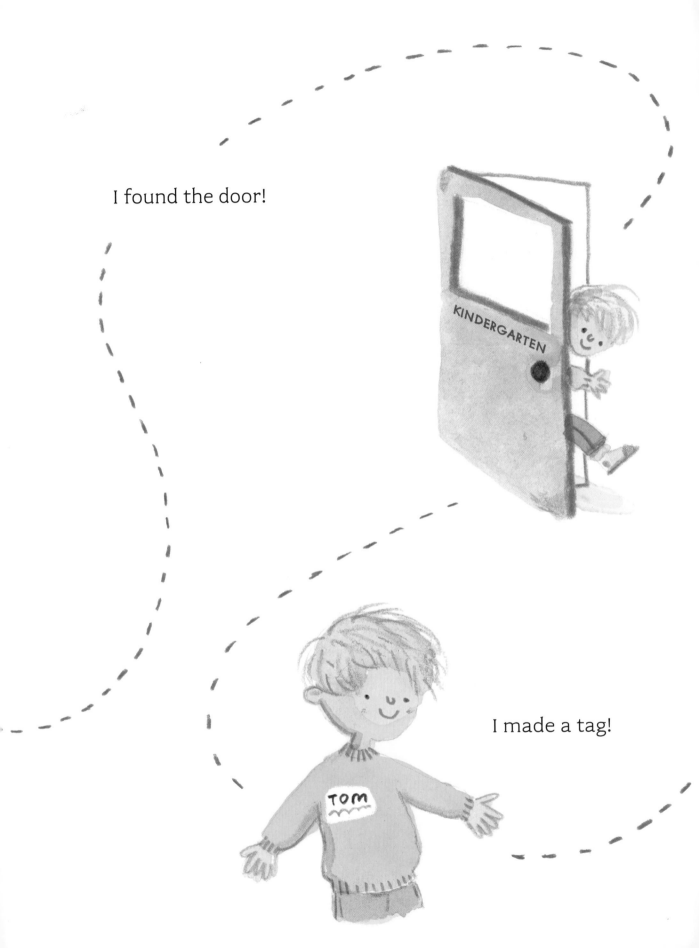

I found the door!

I made a tag!

I painted and glued—
made a mask from a bag!

I read . . .

and played!

I ate my lunch!

I made a friend—
I made a *bunch!*

Kindergarten started

TODAY!